Mafuta the Baby Hippo
by
Betty Misheiker

Illustrated by Ilona Suschitzky

©Betty Misheiker Publications

www.bettymisheiker.com

Mafuta, the baby hippopotamus was a fat little baby hippo, born on the banks of a wide, muddy river that flowed through the heart of Kwazulu-Natal. Because he was such a round fat little baby, his mother decided to call him Mafuta, which is something like 'Fatty', in Zulu.

When the baby hippo was a few days old, his mother looked at him and said, "Come along little Mafuta, Follow Mama into the water."

"Oh… it's lovely and cool," replied Mafuta, as he slipped and slithered down the muddy bank and plunged into the river.

"Yes, it is always nice here," said Mama, "That is why we picked this part of the river as our own hippo pool… Now follow me, for all around us you will soon see our whole happy hippo family… all your Uncles and your Aunts… and your cousins… and this is where you must stay, to be safe and sound."

"WHERE ARE THEY…?" asked Mafuta, looking this way and that "I can't see anybody? "Suddenly two

pink ears appeared above the water,
followed by a pair of eyes, and then,
the whole huge head of his daddy
hippo rose into sight with a big
watery snort. "You'll see them in a
moment, when they come up for air,"
said his Mother. "Aaah! here is your
Daddy now."
"Ahhhh… Mafuta… my boy…
welcome into our hippo pool,"
said Daddy Hippo. "Now see that
you behave nicely Mafuta for here
come all yourAunties and Uncles.

Suddenly, right around Mafuta, more hippo heads began rising from under the muddy water.

"Ohhhhhh….. isn't he a little darling…" Said one of the Aunties.

"Ho Ho… a FINE boy… a BONNY boy" Said an Uncle. "What a BEAUTIFUL baby hippo!" Said another Uncle.

"Why… he's just like a little barrel," said the first Uncle. "You mark my words, all of you, Mafuta is going to grow into the BIGGEST, FATTEST HIPPO in the pool!"

"Oh, do you really think so, Uncle Hippo?" Said Mafuta's mother proudly, "Oh, how kind of you to say so."

"Yes yes, I'm sure he'll be the handsomest hippo in the whole river!" Said the Uncle, nudging little Mafuta with his nose. "But… you must eat my boy… eat, eat, eat, eat… and grow big… and fat… and strong!"

Then, as if at a signal, all the hippos went under again leaving only a few bubbles on the surface of the water, as a sign of where they had been. Each day, as he swam around in the pool, Mafuta saw many different kinds of animals coming down to the river's edge to drink. There were TALL Giraffe, who had to bend their knees and stretch their long necks down into the water, to drink. Now and then, a spotted Hyena came slinking along, or a herd of nervous Zebra, who ran away at the slightest rustle of a leaf. Everyone came slowly and carefully to drink water at the river, twitching their ears and sniffing the air, in case

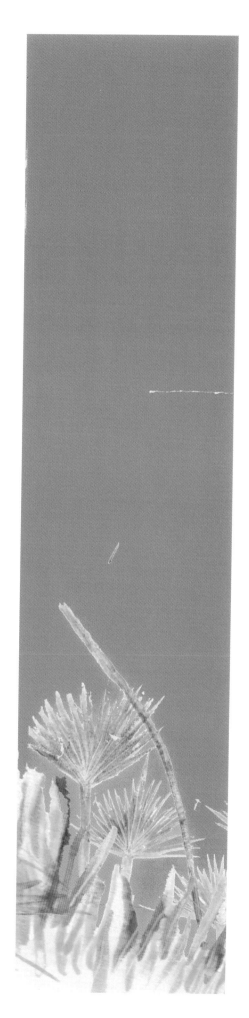

a lion or a leopard was hiding in the
tangled grass on the riverbanks, from
where they could spring out suddenly
and catch the animals whilst they
were off-guard and drinking water.

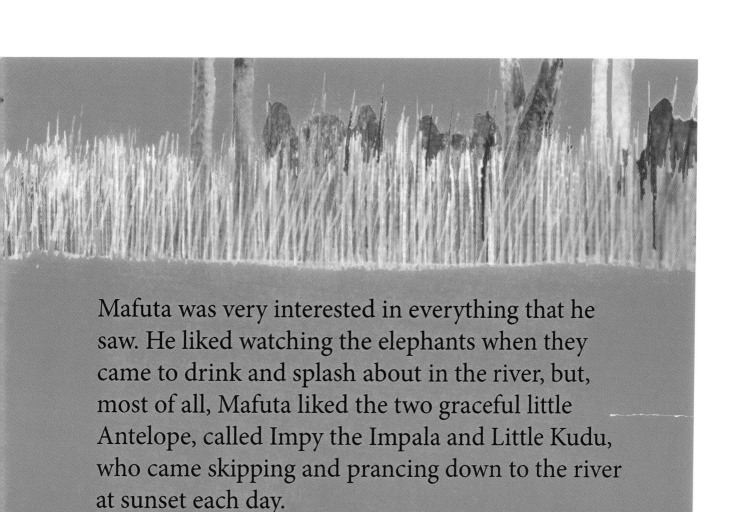

Mafuta was very interested in everything that he saw. He liked watching the elephants when they came to drink and splash about in the river, but, most of all, Mafuta liked the two graceful little Antelope, called Impy the Impala and Little Kudu, who came skipping and prancing down to the river at sunset each day.

Mafuta longed to play with them and decided to float along to where they were drinking and try to make friends with them. Out of the water climbed Mafuta, the Baby Hippo, and waddled over to the two Buck. "Hello…" Said Mafuta. "Can I come and play with you?"

Oh dear, instead of saying "Hello," politely, as they should have done, Impy and Little Kudu stared at Mafuta's fat, grey, TUBBY little barrel of a body and his SHORT legs and his four webbed toes, like a duck, on each foot. They looked at his TINY ears and LITTLE eyes and his BIG face, and do you know what those two unkind little antelope did? "We don't want to play with you!" Impy said. "You look too funny" And little Kudu, just nodded and sniggered.

" I...I...I can swim like anything" Mafuta told them.

"So.. who CARES about swimming... You're SO

FAT!" Said Impy.

"Yes, I know " Said Mafuta proudly "I'm going to be the FATTEST hippo in our hippo pool!"

"Tee-hee-hee" The two little buck giggled.

"What else can you do?" Asked Little Kudu.

"I … I… I… I can walk along the river bed, right UNDER the water for a…b..b…bout a HUNDRED THOUSAND MILES," said Mafuta.

"Fibber… you CAN'T even" Said Little Kudu.

"I CAN… I CAN…" Insisted Mafuta "And… I can hold my breath under water for a loo-oo-ng time too!"

"Go on… tell us… FOR HOW
LONG?" Echoed Little Kudu.
Mafuta twitched his little
ears unhappily, "For…a..a.
HUNDRED THOUSAND
MILLION YEARS."

"Pooh!… That's not even a long time!" Impy said.
The two little antelope started whispering and
laughing and made up a song with which to tease
Mafuta.
"Mafuta, Mafuta you're much too fat…
Do you know… Do you know…
Do you know THAT?
Mafuta, Mafuta, you really ought..
to grow longer legs because
yours are TOO SHORT!
Mafuta Mafuta everything's wrong,
Your ears are too short
and your face is too LONG!"
(Tee hee hee hee….)

Poor Mafuta blinked his little eyes. He felt sad enough to cry, but instead, he did something MUCH better.

"I don't care WHAT you say" Mafuta told them, "You may be very pretty OUTSIDE b...b...b..but, if you're all nasty and mean

INSIDE, then… then… what's the good of
being pretty?… And… everybody says...
I'm going to be the BIGGEST, FATTEST,
MOST BEAUTIFUL-EST hippopotamus in the
whole river... so waaaaaahhhh! I don't want to
play with you either!"

Mafuta waddled back to the river and feeling
very sad, he swam away. Impy and Little Kudu
remained standing on the banks of the river,
watching Mafuta. For a while, they somehow
felt sort of all nasty and mean inside, and rather
sorry for all the unkind things they had said…
but… after a few hours they forgot all about it.

As the sun was going down the next day, Impy and little Kudu, who had been playing together all day, decided to go down to the river for a drink of water. Without stopping to sniff the air, or listen for rustling in the grass, as they had been taught, they trotted noisily down to the waters edge and began to drink. Suddenly, Impy jerked his head up, twitched his ears and sniffed, "Look out! "He warned, " I think there are lion or leopard in the grass behind us."

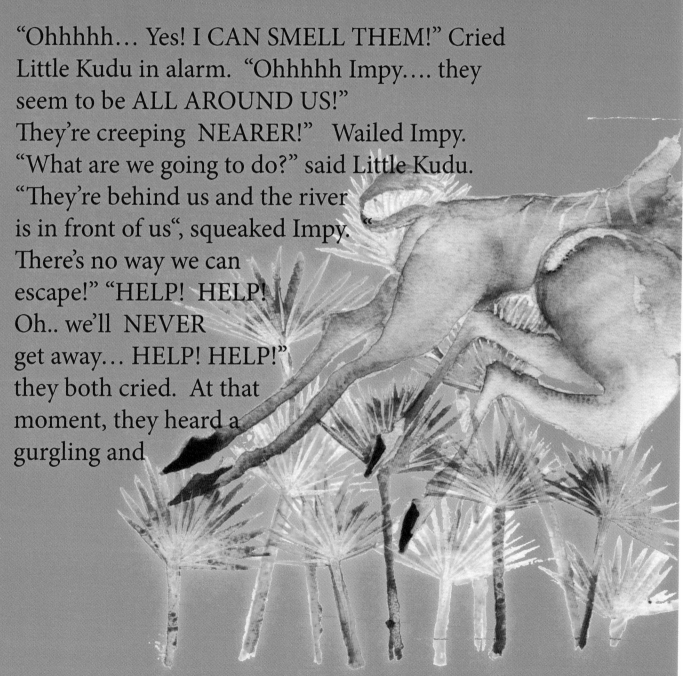

"Ohhhhh… Yes! I CAN SMELL THEM!" Cried
Little Kudu in alarm. "Ohhhhh Impy…. they
seem to be ALL AROUND US!"
They're creeping NEARER!"   Wailed Impy.
"What are we going to do?" said Little Kudu.
"They're behind us and the river
is in front of us", squeaked Impy. "
There's no way we can
escape!" "HELP! HELP!
Oh.. we'll NEVER
get away… HELP! HELP!"
they both cried. At that
moment, they heard a
gurgling and

a puffing and a blowing and a bubbling…
and right in front of them, up popped
Mafuta, from under the water.

"Quick.. jump up onto my BIG, FAT,
BROAD BACK" Said Mafuta, "Come on..
jump! Hurry… I'll take you down the river
right away.   Don't be frightened, JUMP!"
Onto Mafuta's back jumped Little Kudu and
Impy just as the two lions, roaring angrily,
sprang out of the grass from where they'd
been hiding. But, Mafuta just floated away
down the river, as light as a feather, carrying
the two little antelope who were standing on
his back.

"Oh Mafuta, thank you… you saved our lives!"
Said Impy. "We're sorry we were so nasty to you
the other day."
"We'll NEVER laugh at you again for being so
fat." said Little Kudu. "If you weren't so big and
fat." why… you never would have been able to
save us".
"Ahhh… that's alright…" said Mafuta, "…and do
you know what?"
"WHAT?" asked Little Kudu and Impy together.
"I can't REALLY hold my breath for a
HUNDRED THOUSAND MILLION YEARS…"
said Mafuta.

"You can't?" asked Impy.

"No… I was just telling fibs," said Mafuta. "But grown-up hippos like my daddy can stay under water for SIX WHOLE MINUTES."

"Gosh, that's a long time" Said Little Kudu.

"They must be VERY CLEVER!" Said Impy. Further and further down the river floated Mafuta, until they were safe and far away from the lions. The two little antelopes hopped off Mafuta's back.

From that day onwards, Mafuta became their best friend.   For, Mafuta had taught them that, IT ISN'T THE WAY YOU LOOK… BUT THE WAY YOU BEHAVE THAT REALLY MATTERS!

Besides, as far as hippos were concerned, everyone wanted to be the biggest, fattest, most beautiful-est hippo in the hippo pool.

Oh look!
The hippos are happy,
they're happy all day,
With an oom-papa-haa,
and an oom-papa-hey ,
Oh, the hippos are fat,
in the funniest way
With an oom-papa, oom-papa-hay!
They stay in the water
the whole day you know,
Coming up only to puff and to blow,

But as soon as the moon comes up
over the trees,
The hippos come out,
with the greatest of ease.
On the banks of the river,
each evening they play
With an oom-papa-haa,
and an oom-papa-hey !
They stamp and they whirl,
as they waltz on their way ,
With an oom-papa, oom-papa-hay,
With an oom-papa, oom-papa-hay!

THE END

More **African Tales:**

- Nyati, the Big Bad Buffalo

- Stranger in the Forest

- A New Coat for Bunny Boy

- Chubby Roars the Loudest Roar

23822423R00018

Made in the USA
Lexington, KY
28 June 2013